For Bronte-Lou

What's Wrong, Speedy?

怎麼啦？小快

Jill McDougall 著

王祖民 繪

Julie played her new Big *Hits CD.

Then she watched Speedy.

He sat on his rock. He didn't move.

Julie played the CD louder.

Speedy still didn't move.

Julie danced about the room, up and down and all around.

Speedy *still didn't move.

Julie danced about the room and
sang to the Big Hits CD. She sang
very loudly.

This time Speedy moved.

*Clunk! He went into his

*shell.

Julie went to see Mom.

"Speedy doesn't seem happy," she said. "He doesn't swim, he doesn't eat, he doesn't move."

"Give him something new to eat," said Mom.

Julie went to the shop and got some *grapes.

She put the grapes in Speedy's tank.

Then she sat by the tank and watched him.

Speedy sat on his rock.

He looked at the grapes, but he didn't eat them.

He still didn't seem happy.

Julie went to see Dad.

"Speedy doesn't seem happy," she said. "He doesn't swim, he doesn't eat, he doesn't move."

"Give him something new to sit on," said Dad.

Julie went to the pet shop and got some river *stones.

She put the stones in Speedy's tank.

Then she sat by the tank and watched him.

Speedy sat on his rock.

He looked at the stones but he didn't sit on them.

He still didn't seem happy.

Julie went to see *Nanna.

"Speedy doesn't seem happy," she said. "He doesn't swim, he doesn't eat, he doesn't move."

"Take him outside," said Nanna.

Julie put Speedy's tank outside in the sun.
Then she sat by his tank and watched him.
Speedy sat on his rock and didn't move. He
seemed less happy than ever.

17

Julie went to see *Pop.

"Speedy doesn't seem happy," she said. "He doesn't swim, he doesn't eat, he doesn't move."

"Put something new in his tank," said Pop.

Julie went to the *pet shop and got a *mirror.

She put the mirror in Speedy's tank.

Then she sat by the tank and watched him.

Speedy sat on his rock. He didn't swim, he didn't eat. Then he saw the mirror.

He went to the mirror and looked in. He looked to the right. He looked to the left. He looked behind the mirror.

Julie had an idea.

"I think I know what's wrong with Speedy,"
she said to Mom.

She went to the pet shop and came back with something new.

She put the new something in Speedy's tank.

Then she sat by the tank and watched him.

Speedy looked at the new something. Then he slid into the water and swam about the tank, up and down and all around. Then he ate three grapes and an old *snail.

He seemed very very happy.

Julie put on her Big Hits CD and danced around the room. She was very happy, too.

It would be fun to have TWO pet turtles.

生字表

adv.= 副詞， n.= 名詞， v.= 動詞

故事中譯

p.2

茱莉坐在小快的飼養箱旁，看著小快坐在石頭上。他不游泳，也不吃東西，而且一動也不動。

p.3

小快看起來一點也不快樂。茱莉說：
「小快，你怎麼了？」

p.4

茱莉播放她最新的熱門音樂精選CD。
然後她又看看小快。
小快坐在他的石頭上，一動也不動。
茱莉把音樂調得更大聲。
小快仍然不動。

p.6

茱莉在房裡跳舞，上上下下的四處跳來跳去。
小快還是不動。

29

p.7

茱莉在房裡一邊跳舞，一邊跟著熱門音樂唱著，唱得好大聲。

這回小快動了。

「咚！」的一聲，他縮回自己的殼裡去了。

p.8

茱莉跑去找媽媽。

她說：「小快看起來好像不太快樂耶。他不游泳，也不吃東西，而且一動也不動。」

媽媽說：「給他點新東西吃吃看。」

p.9

茱莉跑到商店裡買了一些葡萄。

她把葡萄放到小快的飼養箱裡，然後坐在飼養箱旁看著他。

p.10

小快坐在他的石頭上。他看著那些葡萄，但是卻沒有吃它們。

他看起來好像還是不快樂。

p.12

茱莉跑去找爸爸。

她說：「小快看起來好像不太快樂耶，他不游泳，也不吃東西，而且一動也不動。」

爸爸說：「給他點新東西坐坐看。」

p.13

茱莉跑到寵物店裡，買了一些新的河石。

她把河石放到小快的飼養箱裡，然後坐在飼養箱旁看著他。

p.14

小快坐在他的石頭上。他看著那些河石，但是卻沒有跑去坐在上面。

他看起來好像還是不快樂。

p.16

茱莉跑去找奶奶。

她說：「小快看起來好像不太快樂耶，他不游泳，也不吃東西，而且一動也不動。」

奶奶說：「帶他去外面看看。」

p.17

茱莉把小快的飼養箱拿到外面，放在太陽下，然後坐在飼養箱旁看著他。

小快坐在他的石頭上一動也不動。他看起來比以前更不快樂了。

p.18

茱莉跑去找爺爺。

她說：「小快看起來好像不太快樂耶，他不游泳、不吃東西、而且一動也不動。」

爺爺說：「在他的飼養箱裡擺點新東西看看。」

p.19

茱莉跑到寵物店裡，買了一面鏡子。她把鏡子放到小快的飼養箱裡，然後坐在飼養箱旁看著他。

p.20

小快坐在他的石頭上，既不游泳，也不吃東西。然後，他看到了那面鏡子。

他走到鏡子前面，往鏡子裡看。他右看看，左看看，還看了看鏡子後面。

p.22

茱莉想到了一個好主意。

她跟媽媽說:「我想我知道小快怎麼了。」

p.23

她跑到寵物店裡，帶回一樣新東西。

她把這個新東西放進小快的飼養箱裡，然後坐在飼養箱旁看著他。

p.24-p.25

小快看著這個新東西，然後滑進水裡，在飼養箱裡上上下下到處游來游去。接著，他還吃了三顆葡萄跟一隻老蝸牛。

他看起來好快樂好快樂。

p.26

茱莉播放著她的熱門音樂精選 CD ，還在房間裡到處跳舞。她也好快樂好快樂。

有了兩隻寵物龜，以後的日子一定會很好玩。

句ㄐㄩ 型ㄒㄧㄥˊ 練ㄌㄧㄢˋ 習ㄒㄧˊ

Someone Didn't....

　　在ㄗㄞˋ「怎ㄗㄣˇ 麼ㄇㄜ˙ 了ㄌㄜ˙ ，小ㄒㄧㄠˇ 快ㄎㄨㄞˋ ?」故ㄍㄨˋ 事ㄕˋ 中ㄓㄨㄥ ，有ㄧㄡˇ 許ㄒㄩˇ 多ㄉㄨㄛ 關ㄍㄨㄢ 於ㄩˊ "Speedy didn' t...."（小ㄒㄧㄠˇ 快ㄎㄨㄞˋ 不ㄅㄨˋ ……）的ㄉㄜ˙ 用ㄩㄥˋ 法ㄈㄚˇ ，現ㄒㄧㄢˋ 在ㄗㄞˋ 我ㄨㄛˇ 們ㄇㄣ˙ 就ㄐㄧㄡˋ 一ㄧ 起ㄑㄧˇ 來ㄌㄞˊ 練ㄌㄧㄢˋ 習ㄒㄧˊ "Someone didn' t...."（某ㄇㄡˇ 人ㄖㄣˊ 不ㄅㄨˋ ……）的ㄉㄜ˙ 句ㄐㄩˋ 型ㄒㄧㄥˊ 吧ㄅㄚ˙ ！

① 請ㄑㄧㄥˇ 跟ㄍㄣ 著ㄓㄜ˙ CD 的ㄉㄜ˙ Track 4，唸ㄋㄧㄢˋ 出ㄔㄨ 下ㄒㄧㄚˋ 面ㄇㄧㄢˋ 這ㄓㄜˋ 些ㄒㄧㄝ 表ㄅㄧㄠˇ 示ㄕˋ「動ㄉㄨㄥˋ 作ㄗㄨㄛˋ 」的ㄉㄜ˙ 英ㄧㄥ 文ㄨㄣˊ ：

read a book

go to the park

take a bus

dance

climb a tree

play basketball

② 請仔細聽 CD 的 Track 5，利用左頁的提示完成
以下的句子：

Speedy didn't look happy.
He didn't swim.
He didn't eat.
He didn't move.
I didn't _____.
Barbara didn't _____.
The boy didn't _____.
Helen didn't _____.
They didn't _____.
John didn't _____.

烏龜的群居生活與誕生

　　小朋友，你知道烏龜是喜歡群居生活的動物嗎？牠們的「個性」跟我們人類其實有點像，雖然可以單獨生存，但是牠們就像故事裡的小快一樣，沒有同伴還是會感到寂寞的。所以一般的野生烏龜喜歡一大群一起住在一個洞穴裡，有時候還會因為太擁擠，彼此磨來磨去，磨到背上的殼都變光滑、四隻腳都磨破皮了，都還捨不得分開呢！

　　那麼，烏龜寶寶是如何誕生的呢？下面就讓我們來瞧瞧吧！

　　烏龜是卵生動物，當烏龜媽媽在準備下蛋的時候，會挑選有充足陽光的沙地，好讓蛋能夠保持溫暖。在找到合適的地方之後，牠會先在地上挖一個洞，把蛋孵在裡面，然後用沙子埋起來。蛋的數量跟大小，會依烏龜的種類而有所不同，有些海龜一次可以生 200 多顆蛋，但也有些烏龜一次只能生一顆。在蛋孵化的時候，周圍環境的溫度具有決定性的影響：它不但左右著蛋孵出來的時間（常溫之下大約要三個月才能孵出來），甚至還會影響小烏龜的性別喔！

　　雖然說有些烏龜一次可以生很多蛋，但真正能生存下來的野生烏龜卻不多，這是因為烏龜媽媽在生完蛋、埋完沙子以後，就不會在一旁等牠們孵出來、悉心照顧牠們了，這對於剛出生的小烏龜而言，生存條件相當不利。這些小烏龜在沒有媽媽保護的情況下，常常不幸的成為鳥類或其他動物的食物。這可以說是大自然給小烏龜的考驗吧！

寫書的人

Jill McDougall is an Australian children's writer whose first book, "Anna the Goanna," was a Children's Book Council Notable Book. Jill has written and published over eighty titles for children including short stories, picture books and novels. Jill enjoys yoga, cooking and walking her two dogs along the beach.

畫畫的人

王祖民，江蘇蘇州市人。現任江蘇少年兒童出版社美術編輯副編審，從事兒童讀物插圖創作工作，作品曾多次在國際國內獲獎。作品《虎丘山》曾獲聯合國科教文野間兒童讀物插圖獎。

小烏龜大麻煩系列
Turtle Trouble Series

Jill McDougall　著／王祖民　繪

附中英雙語朗讀CD／適合具基礎英文閱讀能力者(國小4-6年級)閱讀

① 貪吃的烏龜小快 (Speedy the Greedy Turtle)
② 小快的比賽 (Speedy's Race)
③ 小快上學去 (Speedy Goes to School)
④ 電視明星小快 (Speedy the TV Star)
⑤ 怎麼啦，小快？(What's Wrong, Speedy?)
⑥ 小快在哪裡？(Where Is Speedy?)

　　烏龜小快是小女孩茉莉養的寵物，他既懶散又貪吃，還因此鬧出不少笑話，讓茉莉一家人的生活充滿歡笑跟驚奇！想知道烏龜小快發生了什麼事嗎？快看《小烏龜大麻煩系列》故事，保證讓你笑聲不斷喔！

國家圖書館出版品預行編目資料

What's Wrong, Speedy?:怎麼啦, 小快? / Jill
　McDougall著;王祖民繪;本局編輯部譯.－－初版
　一刷.－－臺北市: 三民，2005
　　　面;　公分.－－(Fun心讀雙語叢書.小烏龜，大
　麻煩系列⑤)
中英對照
ISBN 957-14-4327-1　　(精裝)

1.英國語言－讀本

523.38　　　　　　　　　　　　　94012418

網路書店位址　http://www.sanmin.com.tw

© 　What's Wrong, Speedy?
　　　　──怎麼啦, 小快?

著作人　　Jill McDougall
繪　書　　王祖民
譯　書　　本局編輯部
發行人　　劉振強
著作財　　三民書局股份有限公司
產權人　　臺北市復興北路386號
發行所　　三民書局股份有限公司
　　　　　地址／臺北市復興北路386號
　　　　　電話／(02)25006600
　　　　　郵撥／0009998-5
印刷所　　三民書局股份有限公司
門市部　　復北店／臺北市復興北路386號
　　　　　重南店／臺北市重慶南路一段61號
初版一刷　2005年8月
編　號　　S 805621
定　價　　新臺幣壹佰捌拾元整
行政院新聞局登記證局版臺業字第○二○○號

ISBN　957-14-4327-1　　(精裝)